KU-166-738

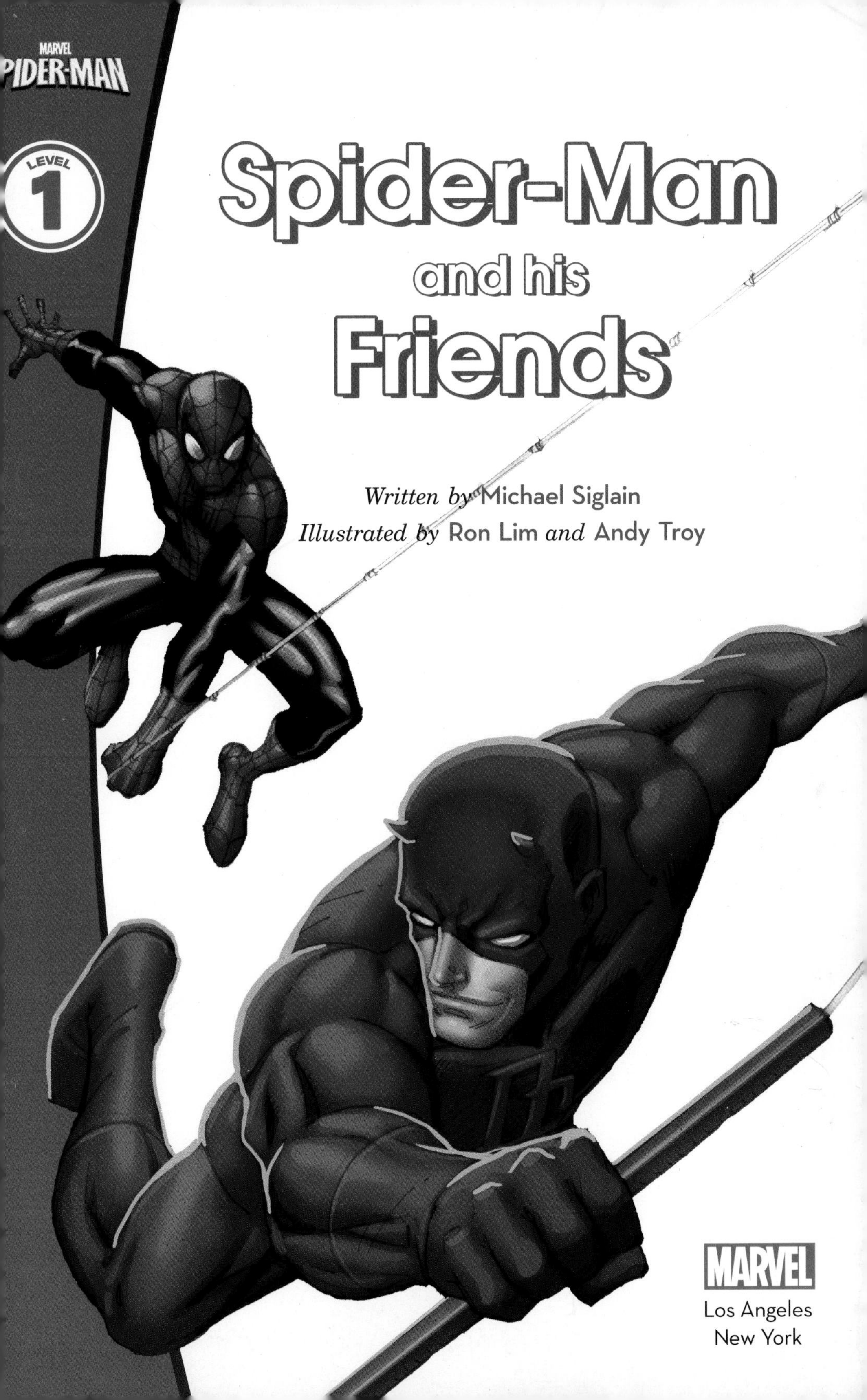

Spider-Man and his Friends

Written by Michael Siglain

Illustrated by Ron Lim *and* Andy Troy

MARVEL
Los Angeles
New York

MARVEL

Scholastic Children's Books
Euston House,
24 Eversholt Street,
London NW1 1DB, UK

A division of Scholastic Ltd
London ~ New York ~ Toronto ~ Sydney ~ Auckland
Mexico City ~ New Delhi ~ Hong Kong

This book was first published in Australia in 2015 by Scholastic Australia
Published in the UK by Scholastic Ltd, 2016

ISBN 978 1407 17166 1

Printed in Malaysia

2 4 6 8 10 9 7 5 3 1

www.scholastic.co.uk

Peter Parker is Spider-Man.
He can swing through the air like a spider.

Spider-Man has special powers.
He uses his powers to help people in trouble.

Spider-Man sees a train coming off the tracks.
He swings into action!

Daredevil has attacked the train. But Daredevil is Spider-Man's friend.

Daredevil tries to fight Spider-Man.
'Why are you fighting me?' asks Spider-Man.

Nova arrives. He is Spider-Man's friend.
But Nova fights Spider-Man, too.

Something is wrong.
They should not attack Spider-Man.

Nova has tricked Spider-Man.
The police think that Spider-Man
attacked the train.

No way!

CHIPS

Spider-Man escapes from the police.
He thinks about his friends and
why they are being bad.

Then Spider-Man sees Iron Man.
Perhaps he knows what is wrong with
Nova and Daredevil.

‘Can you help me?’ asks Spider-Man.
But Iron Man has also become bad,
and he zooms away.

But Spider-Man does not give up.
He catches Iron Man.

Spider-Man ties Iron Man up
and pulls off his mask.
It is not Iron Man but a villain,
called Chameleon!

Spider-Man must rescue his friends!

'About time,' says Nova.

Spider-Man says goodbye to his friends. He is glad his friends stayed good.

Spider-Man saved his friends.
He is a hero.